What's the Matter, Kelly Beans?

What's the Matter, Kelly Beans?

JUDITH ROSS ENDERLE
STEPHANIE GORDON TESSLER

illustrated by Blanche Sims

CANDLEWICK PRESS
CAMBRIDGE, MASSACHUSETTS

Text copyright © 1996 by Judith Ross Enderle and
Stephanie Gordon Tessler
Illustrations copyright © 1996 by Blanche Sims

First edition 1996

Library of Congress Cataloging-in-Publication Data

Enderle, Judith R.
What's the matter, Kelly Beans? / Judith Ross Enderle
and Stephanie Gordon Tessler ;
illustrated by Blanche Sims.—1st ed.
Summary: Until her sister's birthday party,
eight-year-old Kelly, who loves to read and write,
feels that everyone in her family, except her,
can do something wonderful.
ISBN 1-56402-534-9
[1. Authorship — Fiction. 2. Sisters — Fiction.
3. Family life — Fiction.]
I. Tessler, Stephanie Gordon. II. Sims, Blanche, ill.
III. Title.
PZ7.E6965Ke   1996
[Fic]—dc20   95-11337

2 4 6 8 10 9 7 5 3 1

Printed in the United States

This book was typeset in Hawkins and ITC Esprit.

Candlewick Press
2067 Massachusetts Avenue
Cambridge, Massachusetts 02140

To Cheryl,
a wonderful friend,
a wonderful writer,
a wonderful everything

With love J & S

Contents

THE VERY FIRST SATURDAY MORNING

Until last Monday, Kelly had always lived in the old brick duplex on Pratt Road. Now she lived in a white wooden house on Skylark Lane, a short street that ended in a field. The house wasn't new; lots of other families had lived there before the Brennans moved in. But it was brand-new to Kelly. Today was Kelly's very first Saturday in her new old house.

One thing in the new house was the same as always: It was Kelly's job to watch baby Scottie.

While Scottie ate his fruit, Kelly worked at the kitchen table. She hooked her feet around the legs of the chair. Her pencil inched across her notebook.

She wrote:

A VICTORIA BOOK by Kelly Ann Brennan
Victoria had a wonderful family.
Her mother was a wonderful artist.
Her father was a wonderful computer seller.
Her little sister was a wonderful ballerina.
Her little brother was a wonderful cute baby.
Her dog was a wonderful golden retriever.
Victoria wasn't a wonderful anything.
Victoria was moving.

Kelly wrinkled her freckly nose. Writing a book was hard work. Where would Victoria go? She thought very hard.

"Kelly," her little sister, Erin, shouted from upstairs.

Kelly jumped. All her ideas about Victoria slipped out of her head.

"What?" Kelly yelled.

"Where's my tutu?" Erin said.

"*Two, two,*" said Scottie, bouncing in his high chair. He mooshed gooey banana fingers in his curls.

Kelly made a face.

"Kelly," Mom called from the basement, where she was unpacking boxes. "Have you seen Erin's tutu?"

"Look under your bed, Erin," Kelly yelled. She wished her sister wasn't such a kinder-garten baby. Erin's tutu was always under her bed. So was her red sneaker. So was her pink toothbrush. So was her new coloring book. It was hard to share a room with messy Erin.

Kelly had hoped she'd have her own room in the new house—a place where she could write all alone. But she didn't. Instead Scottie had his own room—a nursery, Mom called it. Not fair was what Kelly called it.

Dad came in the back door. He put his base-ball cap on Scottie's head. He lifted him out of his high chair and tossed him in the air. Then he hugged Kelly. "You're a great helper, Kelly Beans," he said.

"Thanks," said Kelly, enjoying the tickly

poke of his mustache. "Daddy, I wish I had my own room."

He smoothed her hair. "I know, honey. Maybe next year we can finish off the attic for you."

"Can we? For sure?"

"If people buy a lot of computers," said Dad.

Kelly sighed. Next year seemed forever away.

She closed her notebook. She put her pencil into her pocket. She would find a better place to write — a quiet place, a neat place, a place all her own. But like Victoria, she didn't know where she would go.

Chapter 2

THE BAD SATURDAY TROUBLE

The front porch of Kelly's new house had a worn spot on the top step. Someone must have sat there a lot before the Brennans moved in. It fitted Kelly's bottom perfectly.

She wished they had a big wooden swing for the two hooks in the roof of the wide porch. It would be the perfect place to read and write her Victoria book. But Daddy said that would have to wait, too. A new old house needed a lot of things — more than her own room and more than a book-writing swing.

Trouble, the Brennans' dog, spread out like an old rug beside Kelly. She scratched Trouble's

ears, listening to the friendly thump of her shaggy tail on the wooden porch.

The air felt soft and sunny; it smelled like cut grass and rosebushes and fresh paint.

It smells like new house and new neighborhood and new friends, thought Kelly. She didn't miss Pratt Road, but she did already miss her best friends, Lisa, Shandra, and Jenny. She wished her friends could have moved with her. Last year they went to the summer reading club at the library. Then they always went to the Dairy Queen afterward. Kelly didn't even know where the library was on her new side of town, but she knew there was no Dairy Queen; Daddy had already looked.

Across the street, under a shady maple, two boys were kicking a soccer ball. She hoped they could tell her about the library.

Kelly waved. Maybe they'd ask her to play. Maybe they'd like to read her Victoria book.

But the boys didn't wave back. How could you make friends with boys who didn't even wave?

Frowning, Kelly went back to work. She thought about what Victoria would do next. She started a new page. She printed some big words. She wrote some long sentences.

The screen door banged open. Erin plopped down beside her. "What are you doing?" she asked.

"Writing," said Kelly. She read:

Victoria packed her suitcase.
She put her pencils and notebook on top.
Victoria was ready to leave.
She rubbed her magic ring.
"Kazap! Kazam! Blue eggs and lamb."

"It's green eggs and ham," said Erin.

"Not in my book," said Kelly.

"Okay," said Erin. She hummed "The Eensy Weensy Spider" and made her fingers crawl up Kelly's arm.

"Stop it!" said Kelly.

Erin made her fingers crawl across Trouble instead.

Maybe the porch wasn't the perfect place to write, thought Kelly. She chewed on the end of her pencil. She *had* to decide where Victoria would go. She wished Erin would be quiet and leave her alone to think.

"Want to come to my ballet lesson? I'm going to learn a sunflower dance for my retitle.

Watch!" Erin jumped up. Her feet made a V. Her arms made an O.

"I don't want to go to ballet. And it's a recital, not a retitle," said Kelly.

"Okay," said Erin. "Why don't you want to come?"

"Because I'm working on my book. I'm going to be a wonderful writer."

"When?" asked Erin. She tiptoed in a circle. The ponytail on top of her head jiggled.

"I don't know yet," said Kelly. Erin probably thought it was as easy to write a book as it was to do ballet.

Erin bowed and plopped down on the step again. She put her head on Kelly's lap, right on top of her notebook. She smiled up at Kelly. "I love you, Kelly Beany," she said.

"I didn't ask you to," said Kelly. Only Daddy could call her Kelly Beans. When Erin called her Kelly Beany, it made Kelly feel grouchy.

Dad came out the front door. "Let's ballet,"

he said, and with his arms in an O, he tiptoed to the station wagon. Daddy looked funny dancing like Erin.

Kelly laughed, and some of her grouchy feeling went away. "Keep Trouble with you, Kelly. We don't want her to get lost," Dad called as he backed out of the driveway.

"I will," said Kelly. She petted her dog.

Trouble wagged her tail. Trouble was eight, the same age as Kelly. Trouble would be going to third grade at Kelly's new school—if a dog could go to school.

Kelly went back to her writing. Now that it was quiet and she could think, she had a great idea, the perfect place for Victoria. Kelly wrote as fast as she could.

When she looked up, Trouble was gone!

Chapter 3

THE EVEN WORSE SATURDAY AFTERNOON

Kelly tiptoed through the house. "Oh, no, Trouble!" She checked in the garage. "Oh, no, Trouble!" She searched in the backyard. Still no Trouble. She walked slowly up one side of the street and down the other.

"Have you seen a dog?" Kelly asked the two boys playing soccer across the street.

They looked at each other. They looked at Kelly. They shrugged.

"Trouble is a big yellow dog. But she doesn't bite," Kelly added quickly.

"No dog," said the tall boy. He bounced the soccer ball on his knee.

"Nope. No dog," said the short boy. He pulled up his socks. He pushed up his slipping glasses.

"Kelly!" Erin yelled. "What are you doing?" She waited on the curb.

Rats! thought Kelly. Erin was home from ballet already. And so was Dad. She'd be in big trouble over Trouble. "I'm talking," said Kelly. "Go home, Erin."

"Talking about what?" called Erin.

"About her lost dog," yelled the short boy.

"Is Trouble lost?" asked Erin.

"No," shouted Kelly. "Go home."

"Okay," yelled Erin. "I'll tell Daddy."

Kelly looked both ways. Then she ran across the street. "Come on," she said, grabbing Erin's hand. "Let's go look for Trouble."

"Trouble! Trouble!" Erin tugged Kelly behind her.

Just then Trouble ran across the street. She disappeared between two houses.

"Come here, Trouble," called Kelly.

Trouble didn't come.

"Rats," said Kelly.

"I'll catch her," said Erin. She raced off after Trouble.

"No, Erin, wait." Kelly ran after her sister, waving Trouble's leash.

"We saw your dog," shouted the short boy. He ran after Kelly.

"She went into my yard," called the tall boy. He ran past Kelly.

"Kelly! Help!" Erin called. "Hurry! I've got Trouble!"

Kelly and the two boys raced around the back.

Big paw prints and little Erin prints dotted a square of wet cement. Erin had both arms wrapped around Trouble's neck. The dog was dragging her across the yard, and Erin was crying.

A man waved his arms. "Out!" he shouted. "Get that dog away from here."

Erin hugged Trouble.

Kelly hugged Erin. She brushed away Erin's tears.

"Look at this mess. I should arrest that dog," shouted the man.

Erin cried louder. "Don't let him put Trouble in jail."

"He won't arrest your dog." The tall boy smiled. "My dad's a policeman. Sometimes he says he'll arrest me, too."

Erin wiped her eyes. "I'm sorry," she said. "And so is Trouble."

"Just keep out of my new cement," said the man. His voice was gruff but he was smiling.

Kelly took Erin's hand. "Saying you were sorry was very valiant," she told her little sister. "We'll go home now. We'll clean your shoes and tell Mom what happened."

"See you," called the tall boy.

"Yeah, see you," said the short boy.

Kelly hoped they meant it. She wondered

what it would be like to have boys for friends.

"What's *valiant*?" asked Erin with a sniffle. Her tennis shoes made squishy sounds when she walked.

"It means you were very brave," said Kelly.

"Are you valiant, too?" asked Erin. She held Kelly's hand.

"Sometimes," said Kelly as she opened the back door.

After dinner, without any dessert, Kelly went straight to her room. She was being punished for not watching Trouble. She lay on her bed and listened to the voices from downstairs. Erin was watching TV. Trouble was watching TV. The two boys were out front playing soccer again. If they were girls, they would have knocked on her door. They would have asked her to play. But boys were different. Kelly realized she didn't even know their names.

She opened her notebook. She wrote:

Pop! Victoria was in a castle.
Fifty princesses crowded around her.
"Welcome," they said.
"I am Victoria," said Victoria.
"Are you wonderful?" asked the fifty
princesses.
"No!" said Victoria.
"Neither are we," said the princesses.
"We are valiant," they said.

"Rats," muttered Kelly.

Chapter 4

A SURPRISING SUNDAY

After church the next morning, Kelly felt happy again. She knew all the hymns at this church. They were the same ones they sang at her old church. And the minister was a lady. She shook hands with all the Brennans. She told Kelly how nice it was to meet her, making Kelly feel like a grown-up.

Then Dad drove past the library. Now she knew where it was. Mom said they could go there this week. Kelly couldn't wait.

When their car turned into the driveway, someone was sitting in Kelly's spot on the porch.

"There's one of those boys who helped find Trouble," said Erin. "Come on." Erin tugged

Kelly across the lawn. "Let's ask him what he wants."

"Erin, I need your help inside," said Mom.

"With what?" asked Erin.

"You'll see," said Mom.

"What about Kelly?"

"Kelly has a visitor," said Mom.

Kelly smiled at her mother, then sat on the step.

"Want to come over and see my new hamster?" the boy said before Kelly could say hello.

"Sure," said Kelly. She called through the screen door. "Mom, I'm going to . . . what's your name?"

"Peter," said the boy.

"I'm going to Peter's house. He lives . . . where do you live?"

Peter pointed across the driveway.

"He lives next door."

"Be good. Have fun," called Mom.

Kelly followed Peter across the lawn and up the walk.

The rooms in Peter's house were bigger than the rooms in Kelly's house. Everything was blue and pink. In Kelly's house there were a hundred different colors.

"Mom, this is Kelly," said Peter.

"Hello, Kelly," said Peter's mom. She was unpacking a box of pink dishes. They were the same color as the kitchen curtains and her nail polish. "How do you like my new kitchen? We just finished painting."

"I like pink," said Kelly. "And I like blue, too," she quickly added. The kitchen smelled of new paint.

Another lady was putting checkered paper on a cupboard shelf. "Hi, guys," she said. She had short, short black hair and a nice smile. "That's Lynette, our house helper," said Peter.

"Hi," said Kelly. She'd never met a house helper before.

As Kelly followed Peter upstairs, a fat gold cat raced down.

"That's Taxi Cat," said Peter. "He hates dogs."

"Oh," said Kelly, thinking about Trouble. She didn't think Trouble hated anyone.

Peter's room had wallpaper with baseball players on it.

"I like your room," said Kelly. "Do you play baseball?"

"My mom picked the paper," said Peter. "I wanted soccer or dinosaur wallpaper."

If Kelly could have wallpaper, she would choose one with books. Reading was her absolute favorite thing to do. Erin wouldn't want books. She'd probably want ballet wallpaper with dancing sunflowers.

Peter went to a cage on his dresser. A pink nose poked out of the wood shavings. Next came a head with two bright eyes, then a roly-poly brown ball. Peter took his hamster out and cupped him in his hands.

Kelly rubbed the tiny hamster head. "What's his name?"

"Dandy," Peter said. "Want to hold him?"

Dandy felt as soft as a cotton ball. His whiskers and feet tickled Kelly's hands. Kelly wished she had a hamster like Dandy.

"Let's go," said Peter. He put Dandy back in his cage.

Lynette gave Peter and Kelly apples to take outside.

On the porch, Taxi Cat climbed onto Peter's lap. Taxi Cat purred so loud Peter almost had to yell. "I'm going to get fish. Maybe a rabbit, too," said Peter.

"Lucky," said Kelly. "I only have Trouble. She's eight, like me."

"I'm nine," said Peter.

"Oh." Kelly had hoped he'd be eight and in third grade.

Taxi Cat stretched and jumped off the porch.

"Do you go to Hepburn Elementary? That's where I'll be going. I used to go to Sunnyside." Kelly paused. "I'm writing a book."

"Oh." Peter didn't sound very interested.

"But my handwriting isn't very good," Kelly said. "So I'm printing."

"What grade are you in?" Peter hopped off the step.

"Third." Kelly hopped off, too.

They threw their apple cores in the trash can by the garage.

"Me, too." Peter sighed.

"How come?" asked Kelly.

"I just am," said Peter. He didn't look like he wanted to talk about it.

"Well, I'm glad you're in third with me," said Kelly.

Peter shrugged his shoulders. "Me, too. I guess. Beat you to your house," he shouted, racing off.

"Not fair. You had a head start," said Kelly when they flopped down on her porch. "Wait here. I'll get my book." She went inside and was back in a minute. "Here." Kelly handed her notebook to Peter. "It's about a girl named Victoria. It's not done, but you can read it anyway." She hoped he'd like it.

Peter stared at the first page. Then he handed the notebook back to Kelly.

"There's a lot more pages," she said. "Don't you want to read the rest?"

"No. I read enough."

Kelly was disappointed. If no one ever read her book, she'd never be a wonderful writer.

"I don't feel like reading," said Peter.

"Oh," said Kelly.

Trouble pranced across the lawn. She flopped on the porch like an old rug, right between Kelly and Peter.

Peter stroked her head. "She's a nice dog," he said.

Trouble wagged her tail.

A blue Jeep stopped across the street.

"There's your friend," said Kelly.

"Tim!" shouted Peter. He jumped up, but the Jeep pulled away again.

Kelly and Peter waved.

Tim waved back. So did Tim's dad, the policeman.

"Peter," Lynette called, "time for lunch."

"See you," he said.

"See you." Kelly watched him run home.

She raced inside. "Mom, Dad, Peter is my friend," she called.

"My friend is Miho." Flour dusted Erin's nose and cheeks. "She's a girl. I'm making her a sunflower cookie."

"Peter and I hate sunflower cookies!" said Kelly, and she went back to the porch.

She opened her notebook.

Victoria looked out the castle window.
A prince waved from the castle tower
next door.
Victoria waved back.

"That's our friend," said the fifty princesses. "We make cookies for him."

"Rats!" said Victoria.

Chapter 5

A MISERABLE MONDAY

The next day, Kelly lay on her stomach on the bumpy couch in her basement. The smell of oil paints tingled in her nose. *Swish, swish* went her mom's paintbrush across her canvas. Kelly was very quiet when her mom had an inspiration. She chewed on her pencil. She wrote:

Fifty princesses led Victoria up the dark stairs.
"Oh, no!" said Victoria when they opened
the door.
Toys and books were spread across the floor.
Socks and shorts covered the rug.
The fifty princesses were very, very messy.
Victoria tripped on a *tutu* poking from under
a bed.
Her magic ring slipped off her finger.

Kelly sighed. Poor Victoria. She closed her notebook.

"How is your book coming?" Mom put her brushes down and stretched. She had as many freckles of blue paint as Kelly had regular brown ones.

"Victoria lives in a castle. She has to share a room with fifty princesses," said Kelly.

"Sounds like fun," said Mom.

"It's not," said Kelly. "The princesses are messy, like Erin. Victoria's magic ring is lost in the mess."

Mom laughed. "Erin isn't fifty princesses, honey."

"She's as messy as fifty princesses," said Kelly.

"I suppose she is, sometimes. But you were too when you were almost five." Mom tweaked Kelly's nose.

"But I never put my tutu under my bed," Kelly insisted.

"You didn't have a tutu." Mom cleaned her brushes and her hands.

Kelly knew that if she'd had a tutu, she would never have put it under her bed.

"Tutus remind me . . ." said Mom. "Would you like to come with us to ballet?" She rubbed Kelly's back. Then she braided Kelly's hair in one long braid.

"Do I have to?" Kelly asked.

"School will start soon. You'll be busy with new friends. And with Erin rehearsing almost every day for her summer recital, I miss spending time with you. Your sister would be glad, too," Mom said.

So she can show off, Kelly thought.

"Writers have to know a lot of things. Victoria might need to know how to dance ballet someday," Mom added.

Not ever, thought Kelly. Victoria hated ballet.

"Can we stop at the library on the way home?" asked Kelly.

"I'm sure we can," said Mom.

Kelly gave Mom a hug. She put her notebook in her room and ran to the car.

At the Happy Feet Ballet School, Kelly and Mom sat on folding chairs.

"Take your positions, sunflowers," said Miss Lily, the ballet teacher. Her long skirt swirled when she walked. She wore sparkly blue stuff on her eyes. Her shiny black hair was so smooth that it looked painted on.

Nine little girls in pink tights and pink tutus lined up in front of the mirror. They stretched their arms out to the sides.

Erin waved to Kelly and Mom. She stood with her feet in a wide V.

"Where is Miho?" asked Miss Lily.

"She had to go to her grandma's," said Erin.

"Oh, dear," said Miss Lily. "Today we won't have a honeybee for every sunflower."

Erin pointed at Kelly. "My sister could be a honeybee."

Kelly shook her head no.

"Brava!" said Miss Lily. She swirled over to Kelly.

"You can do it," said Mom. "Just watch the others."

"Our new honeybee," said Miss Lily as she led Kelly to the center of the room.

Kelly made a face at Erin in the mirror.

Erin smiled.

"Arms out everyone," said Miss Lily.

Erin put her arms out.

Kelly's arms shot out.

"Flutter fingers, flowers," said Miss Lily.

Erin fluttered her fingers.

"Flap your arms, honeybees," said Miss Lily.

Kelly waved her arms.

"Good," said Miss Lily. "Flowers ready."

Erin did her V and O pose.

Miss Lily turned on the record player. "Flutter and bow, flowers," she called. "Honeybees, skip in a circle."

Kelly looked at Mom.

Mom smiled and nodded.

Kelly skipped. She felt like a huge bird, not a honeybee. Then Kelly tripped and landed on her knee.

Someone laughed. Kelly was sure it was Erin.

The music stopped.

"Try again, honeybees," Miss Lily said.

But Kelly was on her way to the car. She

would never speak to her sister again. Never! And all the way home she didn't.

It wasn't until she was getting out of the car that Kelly remembered the library. "You promised," she said to Mom.

"Another time," said Mom. "I'm sorry we forgot."

Rats! It was all Erin's fault, thought Kelly. *Everything was always Erin's fault. Rats! Rats! Rats!*

At dinner, Erin told about ballet. "Kelly fell down," she said. "So I didn't have a honeybee." Erin made an O with her arms and smiled.

Kelly glared at her. "Mom, tell her to stop dancing at the table. And to stop smiling."

"Put your arms down, Erin," said Mom.

Erin folded her arms. Her bottom lip poked out.

"Erin, your sister didn't fall on purpose, and she hurt her knee," said Dad. He patted Kelly's hand. "Your turn to tell us something, Kelly Beans."

As she started to tell about her book, Scottie slid down in his high chair. He got stuck and started to cry.

Everyone jumped up.

Kelly felt as grouchy as a honeybee with a sore knee. "Excuse me. I'm done eating," she said.

Upstairs, she kicked all of Erin's things that were on her side of the room. Then Kelly opened her notebook and wrote:

Victoria wished she could find her magic ring.
For two whole weeks she looked and looked.
She was tired of sharing her room in the castle.
She wished the fifty messy princesses would go to Mars.
They could keep their tutus on the floor there.
They could dance sunflower dances there.
They could stop bugging Victoria there.
Victoria searched and searched.

"Aha!" Victoria had found her ring under a tutu.

"Kazap! Kazam! Blue eggs and lamb."

Victoria escaped from the castle.

Chapter 6

A TERRIBLE TUESDAY MORNING

"Hi, Kelly. Do you remember Tim?" said Peter when she joined them on the curb the next day. "He's eight and a half. He's going to be in third grade, too."

Kelly remembered Tim. She remembered his policeman dad. And she remembered the new cement. "Hi," she said. "Maybe we'll all be in the same class."

"I hope it's Mr. Crane's class," said Tim.

"Me, too," said Peter.

Kelly didn't know what to say. She didn't know any of the teachers. The only kids she'd know at school were Peter and Tim. And she hardly knew them.

"Do you like books?" Kelly asked Tim.

"She *really* likes books!" said Peter, falling back on the grass.

"I was in the Word Busters group last year," said Tim.

"That's the best readers," said Peter.

Kelly smiled. "At Sunnyside I was in the Shooting Stars. I'm writing a book."

"A real book?" Tim looked at Peter. "Is it the kind you get at the library?"

Peter shrugged. "It's just a notebook."

"It's real," said Kelly. "It's a daring adventure."

"It's about a girl," said Peter.

"Can I read it?" Tim asked.

Kelly thought no one would ever ask to read her book.

Peter jumped up. "I know something more fun than books."

"What?" asked Tim.

"Yeah, what?" Kelly asked. "What?"

"Playing with Dandy, my hamster," said

Peter, balancing on the curb. "Come on, Tim."

"All you can do is hold him," said Kelly, not moving. She rested her chin in her hands.

"Uh-uh. You can put him inside his plastic ball. He goes all over the room. Sometimes he runs into the wall. It's really funny," said Peter.

It didn't sound funny to Kelly. "Poor Dandy," she said. "That would hurt."

"Naw. That's how he exercises. He likes it," said Peter.

"Let's go," said Tim. "I'll read your book later."

"Maybe," said Kelly. She wasn't going to count on it.

"Kelly, come home. I need you," called her mom.

The boys raced away, leaving Kelly alone.

What she really needed was an eight-year-old girl in the third grade to move to Skylark Lane.

"Mom, can I phone my old friends?" Kelly asked as she let the back door bang. "Please."

"Later, honey," said her mother. "Right now I really need you to keep an eye on Scottie. Your dad wants a hand with his project. Afterward, if you like, we can go to the library."

"Okay! Can I get seven books?"

"As many as you like," said Mom. She handed Scottie and Kelly some orange wedges.

While Kelly watched her little brother eat, she wrote in her book:

Victoria was lonesome.
She decided to go to the library.

Chapter 7

THE TOUGHER TUESDAY AFTERNOON

Kelly had finished reading two library books when Peter and Tim came over. Now they were all playing computer games in Kelly's room. Tim said the games were easy. Peter said they were hard. Kelly and Tim had to beg him to let them play. It seemed that Peter never wanted to do anything except play with his hamster.

Kelly concentrated on the screen. She pretended she was Victoria. The dragon lunged. His flames didn't even touch her. Victoria jumped and made the perilous leap over the deep dark pit. Next she flashed like lightning through the castle's maze and up the towering tower. Then, disguised as the Valiant Knight, Victoria saved the beautiful princess from prison.

"*Yay*," shouted Kelly. "Fifty points for Victoria and me!" Victoria always won when Kelly played the Valiant Knight game on the computer. If only she could be as wonderful as Victoria.

Erin ran in and jumped on her bed. "Can I play, too?" she said.

"No," said Kelly. "Go away."

"Don't have to," said Erin. She landed on the floor with her arms up in an O. She threw Kelly kisses.

Kelly sighed. Her sister was such a show-off. "Erin! I'm telling Mom!"

"And so am I!" said Erin. "It's my computer, too."

"Take your dumb old computer. We're going downstairs," said Kelly. "We're watching the *Wizard of Oz* tape."

"Yeah, let's," said Tim.

Erin sang "Be My Little Baby Bumblebee" as she moved the computer mouse.

Kelly and the boys went to the den.

"What do you say, Kelly Beans?" asked Dad. Before Kelly could answer or sit down, he began pounding on the wall again. "Got to finish this paneling job," he said. "I have only a few vacation days left."

It wasn't fair, Kelly thought. There was no place for her to go. No place was just hers.

"Come on. It's too noisy here," said Peter.

"Yeah. Come on, Kelly," said Tim.

They went to Tim's house. His house didn't look like Peter's house or her house. Everything was white, even the rugs. It wasn't a good house for a dog like Trouble.

"Call a cop! Call a cop!"

Kelly jumped. "What's that?"

"That's just Buzzard. He's our parrot. He likes to yell a lot." Tim turned on the TV and clicked channels.

"Where's your mom?" asked Kelly.

"She's selling houses," Tim said. "My sister's supposed to watch me, but she's probably in her room talking on the telephone. She always is. And I don't need watching."

"A baby-sitter? No way," agreed Peter. He climbed into a recliner chair and tipped it all the way back. "There's nothing good on TV but dumb soaps. Ooh, kiss me, love face." Peter made kissing noises.

Tim fell over laughing. "Oh, yuck."

Sometimes the boys were as silly as Erin, thought Kelly. "Is your dad making cement?" she asked.

"No. He's at work at the police station," said Tim. "He's the captain."

"I wish my dad were a policeman," said Peter.

"What does your dad do?" asked Kelly.

"He sells insurance. He owns his own company," said Peter. "He doesn't even live with us anymore."

Kelly didn't know what to say. "Want to know something good? I got seven new books from the library."

"Stop talking about books!" shouted Peter.

"Why?" Kelly yelled. "I like books!"

Peter took off his glasses. He looked as if he was going to cry. "I don't. I get the words mixed up. I have to go to a special teacher for reading. I hate having a tutor."

"My sister Janelle has a math tutor," said Tim. "It's no big deal."

"It's not?" said Peter.

"No," said Kelly.

"Okay." Peter rubbed his eyes. "Want to do something real fun? Want to wash Lynette's car?"

"Yeah," said Tim. "Cool idea. I'll get our bucket and rags."

"You can get the soap, Kelly," said Peter.

"Did Lynette say we could?" asked Kelly.

"She always lets me," said Peter.

"Yeah, she always lets him," said Tim.

"And if we do a good job, she'll give us a dollar," said Peter.

"Yeah. A whole dollar," said Tim.

TUESDAY TROUBLE!

Kelly got her pink shampoo. She'd never washed a car before. Maybe she'd be a wonderful car washer.

They were ready to start, when Erin and Mom walked over to Peter's driveway. Mom was pushing Scottie in his stroller. Trouble was trying to lick Scottie's face.

"I'm going to ballet," said Erin. She did a ballet jump. Her ponytail jiggled. She pointed her toe and flapped her arms. "Today I get to be a honeybee." She twirled around Kelly.

"Stop it! I'm not a flower," said Kelly.

"Yes. You're a sunflower, Kelly-beany-teany-weany. And Peter is a sunflower. And Tim is a sunflower, too," said Erin. She skipped around the boys.

Peter laughed. "Kelly-beany-teany-weany. She's funny."

"No, she isn't," said Tim. "Get away. I don't want to be a flower." He backed away from Erin.

"Erin, get in the car. Kelly, please watch Scottie," said Mom. "Daddy's in the house if you need him."

"But Mom, I have stuff to do," said Kelly. "I watched him this morning."

Mom sighed. "I know, honey. But Daddy's almost done with the paneling, and Scottie doesn't sit still long enough for ballet."

"He likes being a honeybee," Erin called from the car.

"Bee-bee, bee-bee," shouted Scottie.

"Okay. I guess," said Kelly.

"Thanks, honey. Don't make a mess, kids," said Mom.

"Mess," said Scottie.

"He's cute," said Peter. He took Scottie's hand. "I wish I had a brother."

Erin threw kisses as the car turned down the street.

Kelly stuck out her tongue.

Trouble barked. She started down the driveway after Mom's car.

"You'd better tie up your dog," said Tim.

Kelly got the leash from her garage. She and Tim tied Trouble to Scottie's stroller.

"Let's wash the car now," said Kelly. She handed Peter the shampoo.

"This isn't soap," said Peter. "It's pink."

"It makes lots of bubbles," said Kelly. "It smells good, and it's better than plain old soap."

"Yeah," agreed Tim. "It's better than plain old soap."

Peter squeezed shampoo into the bucket.

Kelly turned on the hose all the way. Water

splashed all over Tim, Peter, and Kelly. Bubbles floated down the driveway, all around the stroller and Trouble.

Trouble shook, showering water everywhere.

"Bath!" shouted Scottie.

Kelly pointed the hose at Lynette's car.

Taxi Cat shot out from underneath.

Trouble raced after Taxi.

Scottie and the stroller skidded along behind.

"Stop!" shouted Tim.

"Stop!" shouted Peter.

"Stop!" shouted Kelly. She dropped the hose and it flopped around like a snake, spraying water everywhere.

Just as Kelly, Tim, and Peter caught up to Trouble, the stroller tipped. Scottie crawled out into the mud and clapped his hands. "Go!" he said.

The stroller was muddy.

Trouble was muddy.

Scottie was muddy.

"What a mess," said Kelly.

"We'll have to wash them next," said Peter.

"Hurry," said Kelly. What if Mom came home now? She'd be grounded again.

"We'll help, won't we, Peter?" said Tim.

"Sure," said Peter, grabbing the flopping hose.

They washed the car.

They washed Trouble.

They washed the stroller.

They washed Scottie.

They worked very fast.

In the house, Dad was hammering and sawing. Kelly tiptoed in. She changed Scottie's clothes, then her own. She put all the muddy clothes in the washer, but she didn't know how to turn it on. Peter and Tim went home to put on clean clothes, too. Kelly and her friends were drying Lynette's car when Mom and Erin came home.

"You took good care of Scottie," Mom said. She gave Kelly a baby-sitting dollar.

"Lynette said she'd give us a dollar, too," said Peter. "Let's ask her to take us for ice cream."

The boys ran inside, leaving Kelly with the drying rags.

Minutes later, Tim, Peter, and Lynette came out of the house. "Kelly," Lynette called, "do you want to go to the park with us?"

"I thought you were going to get ice cream," Kelly said.

"No time today. Peter has to sign up for the soccer team this afternoon."

"No, thanks," said Kelly.

"Yeah! Soccer," said Tim. "I'll get my ball."

It wasn't fair, thought Kelly. Tim and Peter had each other. She felt like crying. She kicked the rags into Peter's garage, then sat on her own porch.

She picked up her notebook and began to write. Trouble spread out like a rug beside her.

"Want me to read you my book?" Kelly asked.

Trouble whined and closed her eyes.

"That means yes," said Kelly. She read:

Victoria went to the library.
She got one hundred books.
She rubbed her magic ring.
"Kazap! Kazam! Blue eggs and lamb!"
Pop! Victoria was at the prince's castle.
"The prince is not home," said the butler.
"He is playing soccer with a prince friend and
the fifty messy princesses next door."
"Rats!" said Victoria.

Kelly chewed on her pencil. What should Victoria do now?

Chapter 9

WEDNESDAY WOES

The next morning, Kelly was grounded. Mom had found the muddy clothes in the washer. "You should have told me," she said.

"I meant to. I forgot." Kelly started to cry. "I'll give you back the dollar."

"No, honey," said Mom. "It was Daddy's turn to watch Scottie, and you did help Daddy. But I think it's time to show you how to work the washer." She hugged Kelly.

"Am I still grounded?" Kelly asked.

"I'm afraid so," said Mom. "When I come home from the art exhibit, you can play."

Kelly watched Scottie all morning. Even if it wasn't her turn, she'd have done it to help Mom. She read her Victoria book to him.

This time he seemed to like it a lot. He ate a cookie. He said, "Mo . . ."

From her bedroom window, Kelly saw Tim run to Peter's house. He was carrying his soccer ball and wearing his shin guards and cleats. When they left with Lynette, Kelly went to sit on the porch.

Dad pulled into the driveway with Erin just before Mom left for the Duchess County Art Show. "Why the pickle face, Kelly Beans?" he asked. "Where are Peter and Tim?"

"At soccer practice, I guess," said Kelly.

"I'll drive you to the park," Dad said.

"No, thanks," said Kelly. "I'm grounded."

"Uh-oh." Dad ruffled her hair. He patted Trouble.

"Uh-oh," said Erin.

Kelly glared at her. Dad was nice. Nicer than Peter and Tim. And much nicer than Erin.

"Erin, go inside and take off your tutu,"

said Dad. "I'll be there in a minute." He sat on the step beside Kelly. "What's wrong, Kelly Beans?"

"Everything," said Kelly. "It isn't fair. Erin has Miho and her friends at ballet. I don't have anybody."

"You have Peter and Tim for friends," said Dad.

"But they're boys. And they have each other. And they like soccer better than books and better than me."

Dad put his arm around Kelly and hugged her softly.

"Daddy . . . I want to be a wonderful writer. But in my story I don't even know what Victoria should do anymore. And I'm always getting grounded. And Erin never does."

"I know," said Dad. "But I promise you that you'll make girlfriends when school starts. And when Erin's your age, if she breaks the rules, she'll get grounded, too."

"Promise?" said Kelly.

"You can bet on it, Kelly Beans," said Dad. "But I can't help you with your story about Victoria. You'll just have to wait for an inspiration."

"Like Mom gets," said Kelly.

"Just like Mom," said Dad. "You're very much like her, you know."

"I am?"

Dad nodded. "I'm a lucky guy to live with two very smart, very creative ladies like you and Mom."

Knowing she was very smart and very creative like her mom made Kelly feel a lot better.

After lunch, Mom pulled into the driveway tooting the horn. "Everybody come to the kitchen," she called as she came inside. "Gathering all Brennans."

"Come on, Erin," called Kelly. She carried Scottie downstairs.

"*Toof.*" Scottie slurped around the thumb in his mouth. "*Ow.*" He whimpered.

"I know," said Kelly, kissing his cheek. "Scottie's getting a bad, bad tooth. It makes a big owie."

"Major announcement," said Mom when everyone was seated at the kitchen table. She poured orange juice into four glasses and Scottie's training cup.

"What's this all about?" asked Dad.

"A celebration," said Mom.

"What's there to celebrate on a Wednesday afternoon?" asked Dad.

"This is a very special Wednesday afternoon." Mom reached into her pocket. "Look."

"Money," said Erin.

"Lots of money!" said Kelly.

"How much money?" asked Dad.

"Three hundred dollars," said Mom with a little proud smile. "For *Two Daffodils in a Glass Vase.*"

"You sold your first painting!" said Dad. His face crinkled in a big proud smile.

"Can we buy a real wood porch swing now?" said Kelly.

"Yes! A real wooden book-reading porch swing," agreed Mom.

"My mommy is wonderful," yelled Erin. She hugged Scottie.

"*Won-foo,*" said Scottie. He took his thumb out of his mouth. He'd finally stopped crying.

"Scottie and Erin are right," said Dad.

Everyone toasted Mom with orange juice.

"I'm wonderful, too," said Erin.

Kelly doubted that, but she didn't say it out loud.

"I am the sunflower queen in my retitle," said Erin.

"Recital," Kelly corrected.

"That's what I said," said Erin. "I'm the queen."

"Two wonderful people in our family," said

Dad, hugging Mom and Erin in one hug. He kissed Erin on the nose. Then he kissed Mom on the nose too.

"*Won-ful,*" agreed Scottie. He was grinning happily.

"Three wonderful people," said Mom. "Smile, Scottie."

Kelly stared at her little brother. She didn't believe it. There in Scottie's big grin was the bad, bad tooth, sticking up for everyone to see.

All morning he'd cried and cried. Nothing Kelly did had made him happy. And now Scottie was wonderful, too.

"Well." Dad got up from his chair. "I guess I'm kind of wonderful, too," he said. He tossed Scottie in the air and made him giggle. He put his arm around Mom.

Kelly and Erin followed Dad, Mom, and Scottie into the den.

"Ta-da!" said Dad. "Done. All paneled at last. What do you think? Pretty good job, huh?"

"I definitely think it's wonderful," said Mom.

"We're all wonderful," yelled Erin. She put her arms in an O. She did twirly tiptoe turns around the den. "All the Brennans are so wonderful," Erin sang.

All but one, thought Kelly. She didn't feel very smart or very creative. She felt left out.

"Let's celebrate at the ice-cream store," said Dad.

Erin jumped up and down. "I want cherry!"

"How about you, Kelly Beans?" Dad asked.

Kelly shook her head.

"Hey! Another pickle face?" Dad asked. He put his arm around her.

"I didn't do anything wonderful!" Warm tears slipped down her cheeks.

"You don't have to do anything," said Mom. "You're a wonderful helper."

"Me, too," said Erin. "I'm a wonderful helper."

"*Too, too,*" said Scottie.

Kelly stayed close to Dad as they headed for the car. No one understood. Being a wonderful helper wasn't the same as doing something wonderful. She wanted to *do* something wonderful. She wanted to be a wonderful writer. But she needed a special all-her-own place to write while she waited for her inspiration. Just like Mom had a special all-her-own place to paint.

chapter 10

THUNDERY THURSDAY NIGHT

Before dinner the next night, Erin packed her ballet bag. "I'm sleeping at Miho Kudo's," she sang.

Kelly sighed. She used to sleep over with Lisa, Shandra, and Jenny all the time. Now they were having sleepovers without her.

She felt as prickly as a porcupine. Nothing was working out at this new house.

"Don't be afraid without me," said Erin. "I'm leaving my night-light. You can use it if you get scared." She stood on one leg and pointed her toe.

"I'm never afraid," said Kelly. "And quit dancing."

"Okay." Erin pulled a stuffed bunny from

under her bed. "You can sleep with Fluffy. I'm taking Teddy," said Erin. Fluffy had brown carpet fuzz from their old house stuck to her whiskers.

"Oh, gee, thanks," said Kelly, pulling off the fuzz.

Erin propped her bunny against Kelly's pillow. Then she dragged her ballet bag across the floor. She held Teddy by his ear. "Bye, Kelly Beany," she said.

"Bye." Kelly decided she didn't care one bit if Erin was going to her friend Miho's house. Now she could play Valiant Knight for as long as she wanted to. She could write in her Victoria book for as long as she wanted to. She could do whatever she wanted to for as long as she wanted. Maybe she could even phone one of her old friends.

When Kelly asked her mom, she said yes. But when Kelly called Lisa, Lisa's mom said sorry, but Lisa, Shandra, and Jenny were at roller-skating lessons at the rink with Lisa's older brother.

"How do you like your new house?" she asked.

"It's wonderful," said Kelly. "I have to go now. Good-bye." She wanted to slam the phone down.

That night Kelly pretended that she had her own room. Her own room wasn't messy. There was nothing under the beds. She even had her own desk. No one ever did ballet in her room. She could write there without being bothered. And in her own room she didn't need to read any books out loud. She could read all her books to herself. She piled all her hard third-grade library books on her bed, the ones with no baby words.

"Isn't this nice," said Kelly. She read three hard books, one right after another. "Really, really nice to be all alone in my very own room."

Kelly took a bath and put on her pajamas. She lay under the sheets with her eyes wide open. She got out of bed.

"If I want to, I can open the window in my very own room," Kelly announced. She pulled up the shade and opened the window. "And not only one inch so Erin doesn't cough." She opened the window even wider. Kelly got back into bed.

The streetlight made funny shapes on her wall; Kelly turned over.

Thunder rumbled in the distance; Kelly pulled the sheet up under her chin.

Trouble barked in the garage; Kelly jumped.

The shadows in the corner were black; anything could be hiding there.

"In my very own room, I don't have to have the window open at all if I don't want to," said Kelly.

Kelly got out of bed, closed the window, and pulled down the shade. Then she got back into bed and snuggled under the sheets.

"Now my very own room is very, very quiet. And very . . . very dark," she said.

Kelly got out of bed again. She turned on Erin's night-light. She picked up Fluffy Bunny and put him under her sheets.

Then Kelly got her notebook. The pages were getting filled. By the soft glow of Erin's night-light, she wrote:

Victoria went back to the princesses' castle.
The fifty messy princesses danced like sunflowers.

They made cookies shaped like books.
"We missed you," they said.
Victoria was surprised.
"I missed you, too," she said.
But she still wished they were not so messy.

THE NOT SO BAD FRIDAY MORNING

Friday morning after breakfast, Kelly sat in her spot on the front porch. She wondered when the new big wooden swing would come.

Trouble stretched and made a rug beside her. Kelly patted Trouble. She was bored.

Kelly went around the back and Trouble followed. There was a good tree for climbing, but she wasn't allowed to climb trees. Kelly sat in a lawn chair. Then she sat at the redwood picnic table. "There's nothing to do," said Kelly. She could call Peter and Tim, but they had a soccer game. She could read her library books, but she'd read them all — twice. "What do you want to do, Trouble?" she asked.

Trouble wagged her tail.

Kelly sighed. "You don't have any good ideas, either."

Kelly and Trouble went back to the front porch, where Trouble went to sleep. Kelly rested her chin on her hands and watched Trouble. She waited for an inspiration.

Dad was sweeping the garage, and Kelly went to watch. He swept around the lawn mower. He swept under the ladder. He moved the long storage dresser away from the wall and swept behind that.

And then . . .

Kelly had an inspiration. "Daddy! Daddy!" she yelled. "Stop! Wait!" Kelly stepped behind the dresser, too.

"Why, Kelly Beans?" Dad asked.

"I need this little space," said Kelly.

Dad looked surprised. "What for?"

"I need a place," said Kelly. "A place to write my Victoria book. Please?" she asked.

"Why don't you write your book on your computer in your room?" asked Dad.

"On my *and* Erin's computer. In my *and* Erin's room. I want a small writing place of my very own," said Kelly. "Just like Mom has a painting place."

"Let's see what we can do." Dad pulled the dresser out farther. He put shelves at one end. He left just enough opening for a door. "Is this a big enough small space?" he asked.

"It's perfect, Daddy," said Kelly. She went inside and walked around. There was just enough space to write. There was just enough space for her.

Mom and Erin came to see Kelly's space.

"I have a rag rug for the floor," said Mom. "And in the basement there's an extra chair and a little typewriter table that will make a good desk."

"Thank you," said Kelly. She felt as happy as Victoria did when she found her magic ring.

"Can I come in your space?" asked Erin.

"Sometimes. If I say so. And if you are really neat," said Kelly. Erin would never be that neat, she thought.

"Okay," said Erin. She twirled twice. She danced on tiptoes out of the garage. A few minutes later, Erin came tiptoeing back and gave Kelly Fluffy Bunny. "To keep you company," said Erin. "Fluffy is always neat."

"Thank you," said Kelly. She picked a piece

of pink carpet fuzz from the new house off of
Fluffy's whiskers.

Kelly stood in her own space. She lined up
all her pencils. She opened her notebook and
smoothed the page. She sat on her new chair
at her new desk. Then Kelly wrote:

Victoria got her own room in the castle.
Victoria was happy.
But she was still not wonderful.

chapter 12

THE MOST TERRIBLE FRIDAY AFTERNOON

All Friday afternoon Kelly sat at her desk. "I only have two more pages to write, and my book will be finished," she told Trouble. "But I can't think of one wonderful thing for Victoria to do." Having an all-her-own writing space wasn't helping.

Trouble licked Kelly's hand. She didn't help Kelly get any good ideas, either.

"I'll never be a wonderful writer." Kelly chewed on the end of her pencil. She spit out the end of the eraser. She waited for an inspiration. Finally she wrote:

The fifty messy princesses were in a
rowboat.

*A big storm came, and they all fell into
the water.
The princesses could dance ballet, but they
could not swim.
Victoria heard them calling for help.
She jumped into the water, swam out,
and saved them.*

"That's a wonderful thing to do, isn't it?" Kelly asked Trouble.

Trouble yawned and rolled onto her back.

"I guess it would be hard to save fifty drowning messy princesses all at once," said Kelly. She scratched out all the stuff about the boat and the princesses and the storm. Now one whole page of her book was wasted.

Thunk! Thunk! Thunk! Thunk!

Kelly peeked out of the opening between the shelves and the dresser.

A soccer ball rolled to a stop at her feet.

"Throw it here," said Tim. He walked into the garage with Peter.

"Do you want to play?" asked Kelly.

"No," said Peter.

Kelly picked up the ball and held it out to him.

Peter came closer. He looked over the dresser at Kelly's space. "What are you doing in there?" he asked.

"I'm writing my book," said Kelly. "I have only one more page to go."

"What's happening in it?" asked Tim.

"Oh, Victoria is being very wonderful," said Kelly.

"What wonderful things does she do?" asked Peter.

"I don't know yet," said Kelly. "I'm trying to think of something."

"I know," said Tim. "See, there's this big soccer game, and all the guys on the other team are huge, like giants, and they all run as fast as race cars, and they can kick as hard as Batman and—"

"Victoria doesn't play soccer," said Kelly, slipping back into her seat.

"Then Victoria is dumb," said Tim.

"Real dumb," agreed Peter. He gave Tim a high five. "All girl stuff is dumb," he told Kelly.

The boys tossed the soccer ball from one to the other as they ran out of the garage.

"And Victoria thinks all boys are impolite and their ideas are dumb, too," Kelly called after them. "And," she told Trouble, "they weren't very wonderful, either. Oh, rats!

"I wish Victoria had some oil paints. If she came in first place and won three hundred dollars, she would be wonderful. If the castle had a den for her to panel, Victoria would be wonderful. If she had a new tooth, she would be wonderful. But," Kelly yelled at Trouble, "even if she could dance ballet and play soccer, she would still be dumb!" Kelly threw her notebook over the dresser and put her head down on her desk. Now she'd never be a wonderful writer. She'd never be a wonderful anything. Kelly felt so bad that it felt good to cry.

"Kelly, are you here?" Erin called. "I found your Victoria book." She stepped around the shelves.

Kelly quickly wiped her eyes on the back of her arm. "Who said you could come in my space?"

"I'm neat today," said Erin. "I just got back from Miho's, and I didn't do anything messy yet. See?" She held out her shirt and turned in a circle.

"Sure. Fine. What do you want?" Kelly was too mad to be nice.

"I wanted to tell you that Mommy said yes," said Erin. She smiled at Kelly.

Kelly didn't smile back. "Yes about what?"

Erin made an O with her arms. She stood on tiptoes. She danced out of the garage. "It's my surprise. You'll see, honeybee," she sang. "And you'll be happy."

Never, thought Kelly. *I'll never be happy again!*

chapter 13

THE SURPRISING SECOND SATURDAY

Erin's dumb surprise was her birthday party. What a terrible Saturday. Kelly was not coming out of her space. No matter what, she would never come out. She had not finished her book or done anything wonderful. And her only new friends were two boys who didn't like what she liked. Erin was wrong. Kelly was definitely not happy.

"Miho is here," Erin shouted from the front porch. "And Laurie and Charlotte and Kelsey and Carol Sue."

Kelly lay on the rag rug. She rested her head on Trouble. "I don't care if Erin is five and having a birthday party. And I don't care if everybody from Happy Feet Ballet School is coming. I wouldn't want any honeybees or sunflowers for friends." She tried not to cry.

Trouble stretched and got up. Kelly's head clunked onto the rug. Then Trouble trotted out of the garage.

"And I don't care if I don't have a dog, either," Kelly said.

"Kelly," Erin called, "time for the party."

Kelly opened her notebook. She stared at the empty last page and sighed. She shut her notebook. If Kelly didn't go, Erin would tell Mom and Dad. They'd try to be nice, then she'd cry and all of Erin's friends would stare at her, just like that day in ballet class. She trudged to the backyard.

"See my party," said Erin.

All the little girls, dressed in leotards and tutus, danced around the yard.

"You can dance, too," said Erin.

"No, thanks," said Kelly. She picked up a

pink ballet bear plate that had blown off the table. "I don't like to dance."

"Okay," said Erin. "We can play games now." She tiptoed across the grass to her friends. "Kelly wants to play games," she announced.

"I do not," said Kelly.

Clouds as gloomy as she felt scooted overhead.

Now all the little girls were jumping up and down and yelling, "Hide-and-seek. Not it."

"Kelly's it," said Erin. "Cover your eyes, Kelly."

"Daddy always does the birthday games," said Kelly.

Dad was trying to put cups on the table; they kept blowing off. "Thanks for taking over, Kelly Beans," he said, running after the paper plates that tumbled across the grass.

Playing hide-and-seek was dumber than doing ballet or playing soccer. It wasn't even a real birthday-party game. Kelly covered her

eyes. She counted, "One . . . two . . . three . . . four . . . five . . . six . . . seven . . ."

Plop! Plop, plop, plop!

Kelly's eyes popped open as the plops turned to a downpour. Girls in pink tutus ran out from behind the trees, the lawn chairs, and the barbecue. They shrieked and huddled around Kelly.

"It's raining," yelled Erin.

"It's raining," yelled Kelly.

"It's raining," yelled Dad.

"Come inside," called Mom. "It's raining."

Kelly helped Mom dry off all the little honeybees and sunflowers. Their hair was wet, and their tutus were droopy. Soggy leotards and tutus came off and went into the dryer. Each little girl was bundled up in a big bath towel.

"I saved some of the plates and cups," said Dad, dashing in the back door and making wet spots on the floor. "But I didn't get any of the streamers or the balloons."

Erin threw her arms around Kelly's waist. "I can't have my birthday party." She started to cry. "I won't be five!"

"Don't cry," said Kelly. She wiped Erin's tears with a towel. "You can blow out your candles and eat your cake right here in the nice dry kitchen. Then you'll be five."

"Okay," Erin said and sniffled. "But we can't do our sunflower dance, and we can't play any games wearing towels."

"What can we do?" asked the little girls. They looked at Kelly.

"We can go into the den," said Kelly, "and sit in front of the fireplace. And . . . I'll be right back."

"And then what?" asked Erin.

"You'll see," called Kelly.

Chapter 14

SUPER SATURDAY, AT LAST

Snug in their fluffy towels, the honeybees and the sunflowers sat in front of Kelly.

Dad lit a fire in the fireplace, then he sat on the couch with Mom and Scottie.

Trouble spread out on the hearth.

Rain spattered the windows as Kelly read.

A VICTORIA BOOK by Kelly Ann Brennan

Victoria had a wonderful family. . . .

All the girls listened quietly until Kelly came to this passage:

Victoria got her own room in the castle.
Victoria was happy.
But she was still not wonderful.

"Oh," said the little girls.

"Is that all?" said Erin.

"*Mo* . . ." said Scottie.

Kelly turned to the blank page. "Now I will tell you how my story ends.

> Victoria heard a knock on her private door.
> "Come in," said Victoria.
> The fifty messy princesses opened the door.
> "We want to say good night.
> We will not put our tutus under your bed.
> We will not be messy in your room."
> "Thank you," said Victoria.
> She read the fifty princesses 100 bedtime stories.
> "Those were wonderful stories," they said.
> Victoria kissed the fifty not-so-messy princesses good night.
> Victoria was happy.
> Victoria felt wonderful.

"And that is the end of my book," said Kelly.

"Yay," shouted the honeybees and sunflowers.

Mom clapped and clapped. "What a wonderful story."

Dad clapped and clapped, too. "Way to go, Kelly Beans," he said. "You're a wonderful writer."

"*Victoria* is a wonderful book," said Erin. "And you are a wonderful sister."

"*Won-ful,*" agreed Scottie.

"*Woof!*" Trouble barked and rolled over.

"Would you read about Victoria again?" asked Erin.

"Yes, yes," said the little girls.

"Okay," said Kelly. She opened her notebook to the first page. Kelly read:

VICTORIA THE WONDERFUL
by Kelly Ann Brennan